This book belongs to

_____

_____

For Mum and Dad, who made sure that
Father Christmas always found me
J.R.

For the amazing Barney, Joshua, John and Lydia
with love and thanks for being you
T.B.

First published in Great Britain in 2010 by Gullane Children's Books
This edition published in 2011 by

Gullane Children's Books
185 Fleet Street, London, EC4A 2HS
www.gullanebooks.com

1   3   5   7   9   10   8   6   4   2

Text © Julia Rawlinson 2010
Illustrations © Tiphanie Beeke 2010

ISBN: 978-1-86233-822-7

Printed and bound in China

Ferdie's Christmas

Julia Rawlinson

illustrated by *Tiphanie Beeke*

GULLANE
CHILDREN'S BOOKS

It was an ice-bright Christmas Eve, and the sky was
a dazzling blue. Every tree in the wood was frost-sprinkled
and sparkling, and frozen puddles creaked and crackled under
Ferdie's paws. He padded down the burrow-bank where the
rabbits used to live, and bounced over the fallen
tree that blocked their old front door.

And stopped. And looked.
And had a terrible thought. . .

How was Father Christmas
going to find the rabbits' new home?

Ferdie shivered as a chill wind sliced through the wood,
rattling the bare branches. He thought about how
sad he would feel if he had to leave his cosy den.
He thought about how the rabbits would feel
if Father Christmas did not come.
And then he thought about . . .

arrows!

Ferdie began to scrunch around,
collecting sticks from the frosty
ground, making a trail of arrows,
leading to the new burrow.

"What are you doing?" asked Squirrel,
looking down from the branches.
"Making a trail to the rabbits' new burrow
for Father Christmas," said Ferdie.
"Otherwise they might not get their presents,"
gulped Squirrel, and he scampered down
to help Ferdie collect more sticks.

Soon a flock of birds had gathered in the treetops,
their feathers fluffed against the cold,
to see what was going on.

"We're making a trail to the rabbits' new burrow," said Ferdie.

"For Father Christmas," added Squirrel.

"We'll help you!" chirped the birds.

The trail passed between bare trees and
crossed the tinkling, ice-rimmed stream, as the
sun began to set, turning a dazzling gold. Ferdie and
Squirrel shivered with cold and hurried up the
little hill to where the mice were draping
their nest with holly and ivy leaves.

"What are you doing?" asked the mice.

"We're making a trail,"
said Ferdie.

"To the rabbits' new
burrow," added Squirrel.

"For Father Christmas,"
added the birds.

"You'd better hurry,"
said the mice. "It's getting late.
We'll help you!"

So Ferdie, Squirrel, the birds and the mice finished the trail to the
rabbits' new home, which was sweet with the smell of blackberry pie,
cosy and warm. They gathered round the crackling fire, thawing out
their icy noses, nibbling pieces of pie and singing Christmas songs.
And while Squirrel put on a juggling show with holly berries
and mistletoe, outside in the shivery darkness . . .

it began to snow.

Fat white flakes tumbled softly from a heavy sky.

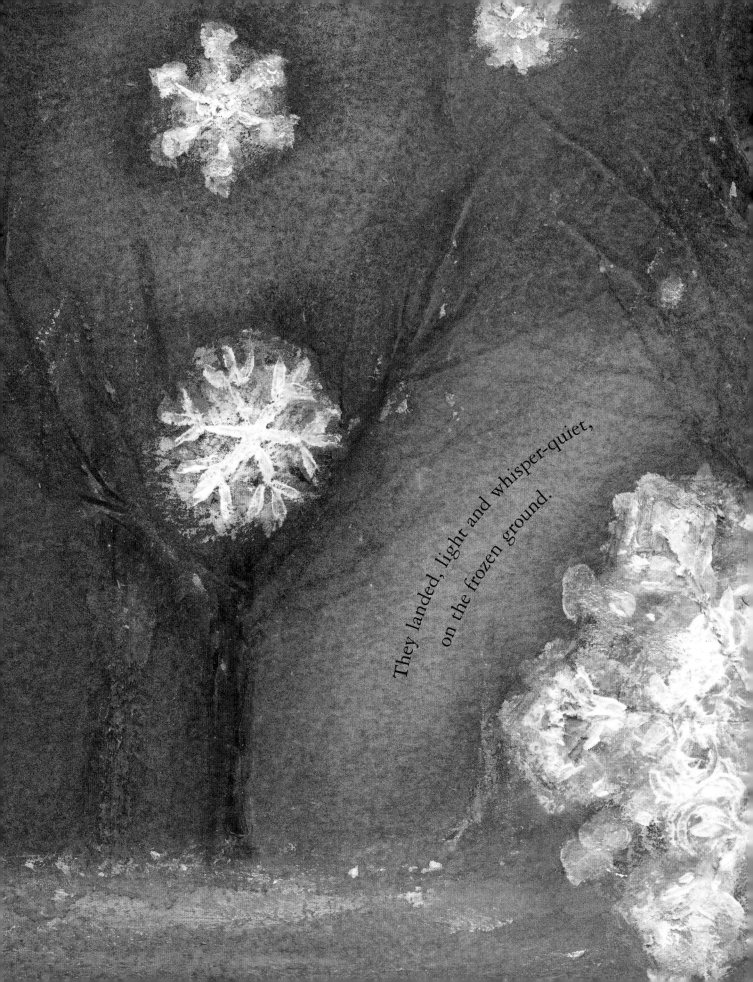

They landed, light and whisper-quiet, on the frozen ground.

And when Ferdie went to the burrow door to go home for the night,
the snow was soft and deep and white, and all the arrows had gone.
"Oh no!" cried Ferdie, blinking back tears.
"What will happen to your presents now?
Father Christmas will never be able to find your home."

Ferdie stared out into the darkness, imagining
Father Christmas lost in the snow.

"I know," he said, gathering his friends.
"If we stay awake tonight, when Father Christmas visits
our homes, we can tell him where he needs to go."
The animals said goodnight to each other and
hurried off through the snow-muffled wood.

Ferdie snuggled down in his warm,
soft bed to keep watch for Father Christmas.

But curled in the cosy
hollow of an oak tree,
Squirrel began to snore.

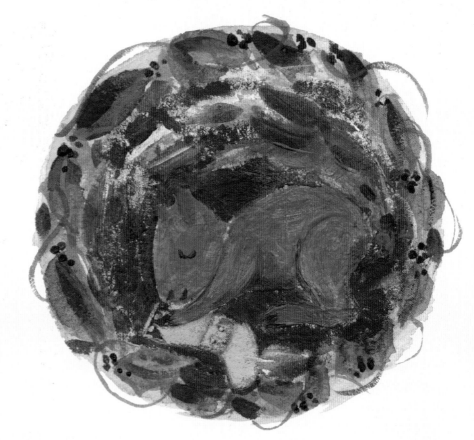

High in the snowy
branches of a fir tree,
the birds began to doze.

In their toasty warm nest,
the mice dreamt of
ribbon-wrapped berries.

And in his snug little bed,
Ferdie's eyes closed.

So when Father Christmas
came to call, everyone
was fast asleep. And next
morning, when Ferdie rushed
to the rabbits' burrow . . .

Father Christmas had found them after all!

"I'm sorry I went to sleep," puffed Ferdie,
"but I've brought you a Christmas rose."
"And we've brought nuts," panted Squirrel, pulling the mice through the snow.
"And we've brought berries," sang the birds, spiralling in the snow-bright sky.

"And best of all you've brought yourselves.
There's room in the burrow for everyone . . .

. . . Happy Christmas!"

cried the rabbits, and they welcomed their friends
into the berry-bright warmth of their home.

Other Ferdie Books for you to enjoy

Ferdie and the Falling Leaves

Ferdie's beautiful tree is losing its leaves. He tries everything he can to save them, but finally the last leaf falls. Poor Ferdie is heart-broken . . . until he comes back the next day and finds a glorious surprise!

'Will make children gasp with delight'
ALA BOOKLIST

'Softly glowing illustrations are perfectly matched with the warm and lyrical text'
KIRKUS REVIEWS

'{A} poetic tribute to autumn and winter'
CHILDREN'S LITERATURE

* * *

Ferdie's Springtime Blossom

When Ferdie tumbles down the hill into the sunny orchard, he can hardly believe his eyes – there's snow on the ground! Off he rushes to warn his friends. But could there be another explanation for the glorious white display?

'Captivating'
PUBLISHERS WEEKLY (STARRED REVIEW)

'Beeke – definitely a talent to watch out for!'
THE SCHOOL LIBRARIAN